Gli Angeli di Alfie

ALFIE'S ANGELS

Henriette Barkow

Sarah Garson

Italian translation by Paola Antonioni

MANTRA LINGUA

Alfie voleva essere un angelo.
Li aveva visti nei suoi libri.

Alfie wanted to be an angel.
He'd seen them in his books.

G

ALF   S

In memory of Alfons,
who taught me about angels. H.B.

For Mum, Dad and Daniel,
for your support and encouragement. S.G.

First published 2003 by Mantra Lingua
Global House, 303 Ballards Lane, London N12 8NP
www.mantralingua.com

Text copyright © 2003 Henriette Barkow
Illustrations copyright © 2003 Sarah Garson

This sound enabled edition published in 2013

British Library Cataloguing in Publication Data:
a catalogue record for this book is available from the British Library.

Li aveva visti nei suoi sogni.

He'd seen them in his dreams.

Gli angeli hanno le ali e sanno volare.
Alfie voleva le ali per volare a scuola in orario.

Angels have wings and angels can fly.
Alfie wanted wings so he could fly to
school on time.

Gli angeli sanno ballare e cantare con voci bellissime.
Alfie voleva cantare per poter partecipare al coro.

Angels can dance, and sing in beautiful voices.
Alfie wanted to sing so that he could be in the choir.

Gli angeli vanno più veloci del vento.

Angels can move as fast as the wind.

Alfie voleva essere più veloce per segnare più goal.

Alfie wanted to move faster so that he could score more goals.

Gli angeli si trovano di ogni forma...

Angels come in all shapes...

...e misura,

...and sizes,

e fanno delle cose incredibili.

and they can do the most amazing things.

Alfie voleva essere un angelo.

Alfie wanted to be an angel.

Li aveva visti nei suoi libri.
Li aveva visti nei suoi sogni.

He'd seen them in his books.
He'd seen them in his dreams.

Bene, una volta all'anno i bambini possono essere angeli.
Le maestre li scelgono.
I genitori li vestono.
Tutta la scuola li guarda.

1920

1941

1963

Now once a year children can be angels.
The teachers choose them.
The parents dress them.
The whole school watches them.

Le maestre di Alfie sceglievano sempre le bambine.

Alfie's teacher always chose the girls.

Quelle più belle. Le bambine con i capelli più lunghi.
Le bambine con gli occhi più grandi e i sorrisi più dolci.

The prettiest girls. The girls with the longest hair.
The girls with the biggest eyes and the sweetest smiles.

Ma Alfie voleva essere un angelo.
Li aveva visti nei suoi libri.
Li aveva visti nei suoi sogni.

But Alfie wanted to be an angel.
He'd seen them in his books.
He'd seen them in his dreams.

Quando la maestra chiese "Chi vuole essere un angelo?"
Alfie alzò la mano.

When the teacher asked, "Who wants to be an angel?"
Alfie put up his hand.

Le bambine si misero a ridere. I bambini ridacchiarono.

The girls laughed. The boys sniggered.

La maestra lo fissò. La maestra ci pensò
e disse "Alfie vuole essere un angelo?
Però solo le bambine sono angeli."

The teacher stared. The teacher thought and
said, "Alfie wants to be an angel? But only
girls are angels."

Alfie scosse la testa lentamente,
e raccontò alla maestra tutto ciò che sapeva sugli angeli.

Alfie slowly shook his head,
and he told his teacher all about the angels.

Come li aveva visti nei libri.
Come li aveva visti nei suoi sogni.

How he'd seen them in his books.
How he'd seen them in his dreams.

E più Alfie parlava, più la classe ascoltava.

And the more Alfie spoke,
the more the whole class listened.

Nessuno rideva e nessuno ridacchiava,
perchè Alfie voleva essere un angelo.

Nobody laughed and nobody sniggered,
because Alfie wanted to be an angel.

Quello era il periodo dell'anno in cui i bambini potevano essere angeli.
Le maestre li preparavano. I genitori li vestivano.
Tutta la scuola guardava mentre cantavano e ballavano.

Now it was that time of year
when children could be angels.
The teachers taught them.
The parents dressed them.
The whole school watched
them while they sang
and danced.

Alfie era un angelo!

Alfie was an angel!